S N O W Y

by *Berlie Doherty*
Pictures by Keith Bowen

Dial Books for Young Readers New York

First published in the United States 1993 by
Dial Books for Young Readers
A Division of Penguin Books USA Inc.
375 Hudson Street
New York, New York 10014

Published in Great Britain 1992 by
HarperCollins Publishers
Text copyright © 1992 by Berlie Doherty
Pictures copyright © 1992 by Keith Bowen
All rights reserved
Printed in Great Britain
1 3 5 7 9 10 8 6 4 2

Library of Congress Cataloging in Publication Data
Doherty, Berlie.
Snowy / Berlie Doherty; pictures by Keith Bowen.
p.   cm.
Summary: When the other children bring their pets to school,
Rachel feels left out because she can't bring in the horse
that pulls the barge on which she lives.
ISBN 0-8037-1343-6
[1. Barges—Fiction.   2. Horses—Fiction.]   I. Bowen, Keith, ill.
II. Title.
PZ7.D6947Sn   1993   [E]—dc20   91-47519   CIP   AC

The art for each picture was done in pastels.
It was color-separated and reproduced in
red, blue, yellow, and black halftones.

Rachel doesn't live in a house, or in an apartment.
She lives with her mother and father on a boat called
a barge, on a waterway called a canal. Her barge is green,
red, and blue. There are castles and flowers painted on it,
and on the buckets and kettles on the roof.

At night when Rachel goes to sleep, she can feel the barge rocking gently from side to side. She can hear the slish! slosh! of water against its sides. Everything inside is small and cozy and bright.

Rachel loves her barge. It's called Betelgeuse, which is a kind of star, but Rachel calls it Beetle Juice. The best thing about living on Beetle Juice–*better* than the rocking at night, *better* than the castles and flowers, *better* than the splish! splash! of the water on its sides–is Snowy.

Snowy is their barge horse.

He lives in a barn on the banks of the canal, and his job is to pull Beetle Juice along the water when Rachel's mom and dad take people for rides.

He's as white as snow. He's taller than Rachel's dad. He has long hair like feathers around his hooves. Rachel's mom puts a bridle on him, and ropes with colored bobbins and jingling bells and shining brasses. Under his tail she hitches a stick called a swingletree and ties one end of a long, long rope to it. The other end of this rope is tied to Beetle Juice.

When Rachel's mom clicks her tongue and says, "Come on, Snowy," Snowy lowers his head and pulls. Then he clop, clop, clops along the towpath, the long rope stretches behind him, and Beetle Juice floats along the canal like a painted swan.

"Please can I take Snowy to school?" Rachel asked her mother one morning. "Miss Smith said we can bring our pets today."

"Snowy isn't a pet," said her mom, brushing Rachel's long hair as if she was brushing Snowy's tail. "He has to work for a living, like me and Dad and Miss Smith."

Then she braided Rachel's hair and put colored ribbons in.

"But can't he have a day off, just today?" Rachel made
her eyes big and round to show how much she wanted to take
Snowy to school, but her mother wasn't looking.

"No," said her mother. "Snowy has to work today."

Rachel cried all the way to school, but her mother didn't
change her mind.

That day Benny brought a gray rabbit that shivered like the grass in the wind. Simon brought a fish with raggedy fins that floated in its bowl like a golden shirt on a clothesline. Yasmine brought a stick insect that pretended to be an old twig.

Benny wobbled his front tooth with his tongue. "Where's your pet?" he asked Rachel.

Rachel put her finger through the buttonhole in her cardigan. "He's gone to work," she said.

They all burst out laughing.

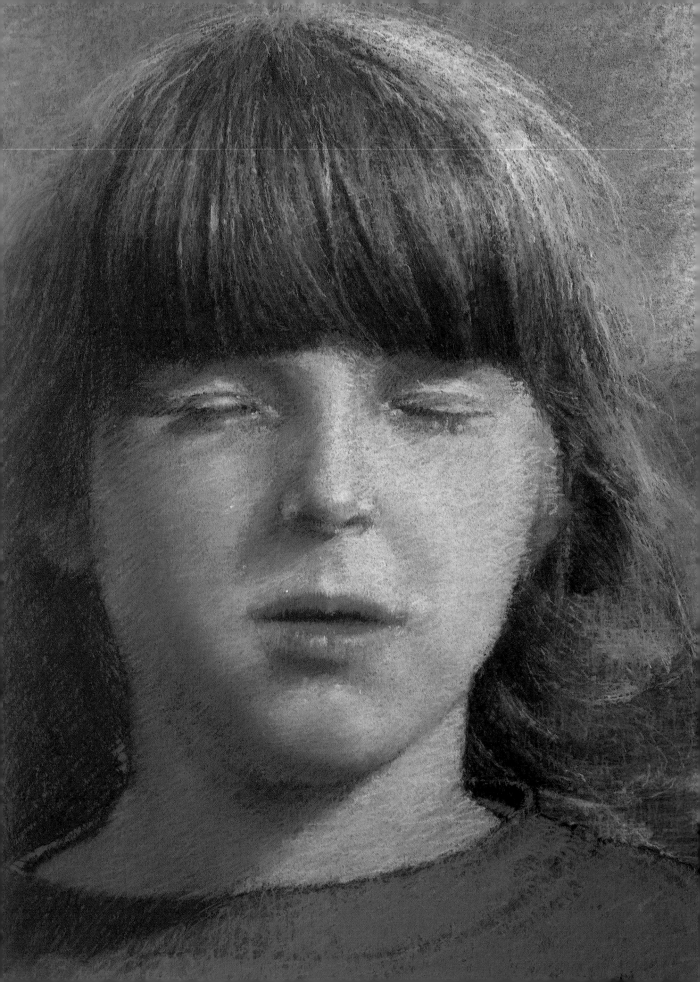

Benny wobbled his tooth again. His tongue squashed in and out around it. "What's he like?"

Rachel closed her eyes. "He's as big as a mountain," she said. "And he's got bells and ribbons and a swingletree. And he smells like a haystack." Everybody laughed again.

Rachel kept her eyes closed. "And he's got feathers around his feet," she said.

"I'd rather have my stick insect," said Yasmine.

Tears began to slide down Rachel's cheeks.

Late that afternoon Miss Smith went to the canal and sat on the grass with Rachel's mother. Rachel's father made them some coffee and toasted muffins in the little kitchen called a galley, and then sat in the sun and visited too.

There were lots of people sitting on the grass outside of their barges. Some of them were playing banjos and flutes, some of them were talking and laughing, and some of them were just enjoying the sunshine.

But Rachel went into the dark barn that smelled of haystacks, and put her arms around one of Snowy's front legs. She rested her head against his soft white side, and cried.

The next afternoon at school Miss Smith told the class that they weren't going to have a story that day. They all folded their arms and sat up straight and promised to be good if they could have a story, but Miss Smith laughed and said they were going to have something even better than a story.

She took them outside, and Yasmine's mom and Benny's dad and Mrs. Lacy the lunchroom cook joined them, all smiling their heads off and full of secrets.

"Are we going for a walk, Miss Smith?" Rachel asked.

Miss Smith took her hand and told her she could help
lead the group. And the amazing thing was that their walk
brought them all the way to Rachel's canal, right up to
where Beetle Juice was moored.

"This is where Rachel lives," said Miss Smith.
Everybody loved Beetle Juice. "It's got flowers painted
on it!" they shouted.

Rachel pulled up her socks and folded her arms and smiled.
Then she heard the most wonderful sound in the world.

It was Snowy, coming out of the barn that smelled of haystacks.

It was Snowy, with his white hair like feathers around his hooves, and his bells jingling, and his ropes and colored bobbins creaking, and all his brasses shining in the sun. Everybody ran to him and gazed up at him with their mouths open.

"Isn't he beautiful!" they said. "Doesn't he smell great!"
Benny wobbled his tooth. "I wish he was mine," he sighed.
"Come on, Snowy," said Rachel's mom. "You've got
work to do." She hitched the swingletree behind his tail,
and tied the barge rope to it.

"All aboard!" shouted Rachel's dad. He and Miss Smith helped the children onto the barge, and Yasmine's mom and Benny's dad and Mrs. Lacy climbed on too.

Rachel's mom clicked her tongue. "Come on, Snowy," she said.

Snowy lowered his head and began to move forward, clop, clop, clop. Rachel's mother smiled and waved to Rachel on the barge. Then she put a hand on Snowy's rope, and walked along the towpath beside him.

The rope stretched out. Beetle Juice, with Rachel and all of her friends on board, began to glide along the canal, slow and quiet and proud . . . just like a painted swan.